This book belongs to

_____

Hi, there!

For information address Disney Press,
1101 Flower Street, Glendale, California 91201.

ISBN 978-1-4847-2151-3
F383-2370-2-14213
Printed in China
First Edition
10 9 8 7 6 5 4 3 2 1

For more Disney Press fun, visit www.disneybooks.com

Do You Want a Hug?

By Kevin Lewis

Illustrated by Olga T. Mosqueda

Disney PRESS

New York · Los Angeles

I'm Olaf.

And I love,

love,

love
warm hugs!

In fact, I am the
KING
of giving them.

So come on.
Let's hug!

I'm waaaiting.

Maybe I should come hug you.

Umph!

Mrfmflm

muffle

mummm

Hmmmmm.
Why didn't that work?

Oh. I get it.

You're playing a game!

If I play a game with you,
will you give me a hug?

Promise?

What game
should we play?

Leap Troll?

Ring-around-the-reindeer?

OH! I KNOW!

I'll hide.

You count to ten,

then turn the page.

Done already?
Count again.
BACKWARD this time!

10   9

YOU FOUND me!

HUG?

Now how
about that